ALADDIN

An imprint of Simon & Schuster Children's Publishing Division

1230 Avenue of the Americas, New York, New York 10020

This Aladdin edition September 2015

For information about special discounts for bulk purchases, please contact

Simon & Schuster Special Sales at 1-866-506-1949 or business@simonandschuster.com.

The Simon & Schuster Speakers Bureau can bring authors to your live event.

For more information or to book an event contact the Simon & Schuster Speakers Bureau at

1-866-248-3049 or visit our website at www.simonspeakers.com.

Book designed by Karina Granda

The text of this book was set in VAG Rounded STD.

Manufactured in the United States of America 0915 LAK

2 4 6 8 10 9 7 5 3

Library of Congress Control Number 2014959030

ISBN 978-1-4814-0619-2 (POB)

ISBN 978-1-4814-0621-5 (eBook)

WHERE'S SANTA?

BRYONY JONES

Illustrated by
CHUCK WHELON

ALADDIN

NEW YORK LONDON TORONTO SYDNEY NEW DELHI

AT THE NORTH POLE

Welcome to Christmas HQ. Over the past year, Santa and his elves have been hard at work preparing for Christmas. It's all hands on deck. But four days before Christmas, disaster strikes! Ten of Santa's elves have gone missing and, without them, everything in the workshop is getting mixed up. Even the reindeer are trying to help, but they're causing chaos.

Santa has to start a worldwide search for his missing helpers. Can you help him spot the ten missing elves in each picture? See if you can find Santa in each picture too. Find the answers plus extra things to spot at the back of the book.

MISSING: Elves

Can you help Santa spot these elves? Look at them carefully, then turn the page and start the search.

Emily
Wrapping Inspector

Matthew
Reindeer Wrangler

Zach
Chief Woodworker

Steven
Elf and Safety

Lily
Battery Installer

Neeta
Address Labeler

Frieda
Novely-Item Wrapper

Mikey
Elf Resources Manager

Patrick
Shoemaker

Rupert
Chef

A SNOWY VILLAGE

The elves can sniff out a steaming mug of hot chocolate from far away, and they've followed their noses to this pretty English village on a very frosty evening.

But while the elves are enjoying a huge snowball fight, Santa is trying to stay out of the firing line. Heads up!

Can you find Santa and the ten elves?

Ye Hot Choc Shoppe

MENU

SAFARI SENSATION

The elves have only ever been to the North Pole Zoo before, so they are amazed by the animals on the safari. The giraffes are so tall!

Santa thinks it's too hot. He prefers the cool of the North Pole. And the monkeys won't stop trying to steal his hat.

Can you find Santa and the ten elves?

CHRISTMAS MARKET MAYHEM

Santa has followed his mischievous runaway elves to a Christmas market in Germany.

They are enjoying the brightly colored market stalls, drinking hot cocoa, and eating yummy gingerbread.

Can you find Santa and the ten elves?

SNACKS

AT THE BEACH

Santa and the elves have made their way to Bondi Beach in Sydney, Australia.

Santa's not used to the sun at Christmas and he's finding his beard to be a bit too hot in the scorching summer sun, but the elves are having an amazing time. Surf's up, dude!

Can you find Santa and the ten elves?

ALPINE ADVENTURE

Anyone for skiing? At a popular resort in France, the elves are putting on their skis and testing their skills on the slopes. Let's hope they're not afraid of heights!

The cold is turning Santa's nose as red as Rudolph's. He's really not a fan of extreme sports.

Can you find Santa and the ten elves?

SANTAS GALORE

The elves are confused. Why is there a whole room of people dressed up like Santa? It's a Santa Convention, that's why.

Santa wonders if anyone would like to take his place back at Christmas HQ. It's hard work getting everything ready for Christmas.

Can you find the real Santa and his missing ten elves?

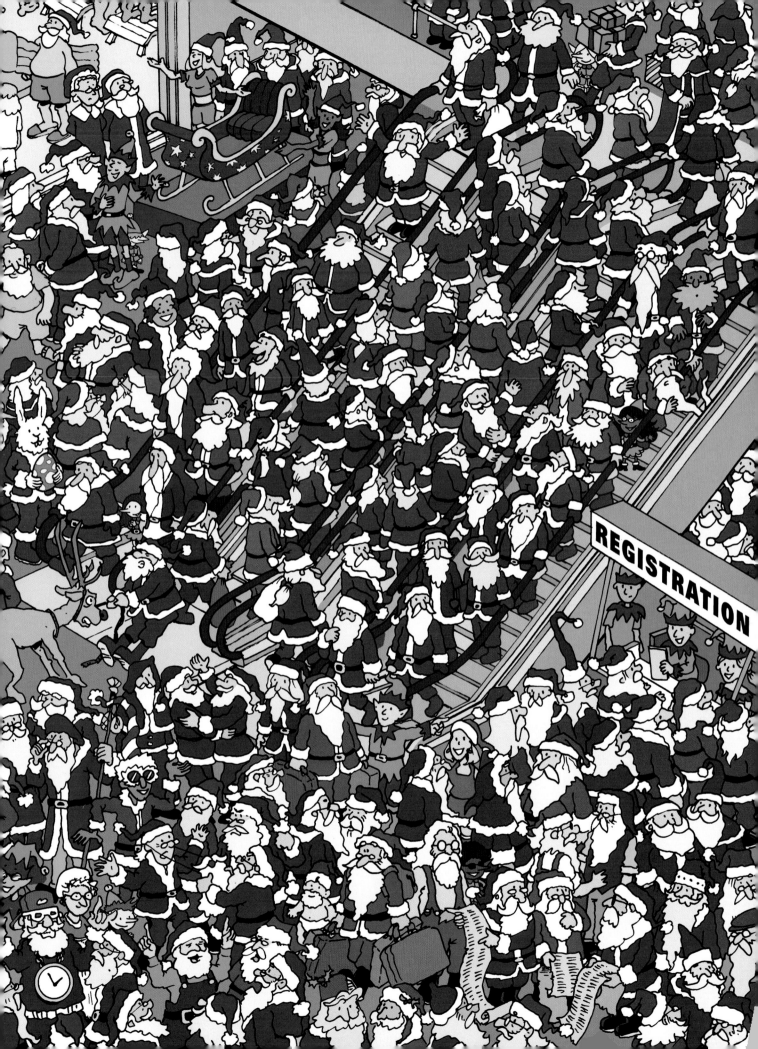

FAMILY FEAST

The elves are stuffed. They've eaten turkey, green beans, and more roast potatoes than there are reindeer in the North Pole. But Santa, well, he's just getting started.

He loves to see the kids' faces when they unwrap their presents. It makes all that hard work in the days before Christmas worth it.

Can you find Santa and the ten elves?

AT THE BALLET

The audience is hushed, the stage lights are up, and Santa's marveling at what's unfolding on the stage. There are leaps, jumps, and pirouettes aplenty.

The elves are eager to learn a few moves so they can show off at the annual elf disco.

Can you find Santa and the ten elves?

FESTIVE FIESTA!

The elves love a good party, so it's no surprise that they've traveled to São Paulo in Brazil.

Amazed by all the colorful costumes and twinkling lights, the elves are lost in the festivities. But with everybody in costume, it's even harder for Santa to find them.

Can you find Santa and the ten elves?

ICE-SKATING

The elves have decided to check out the fabulous ice rink at Rockefeller Center in New York City.

Santa finds the ice much too slippery and prefers to stay on the sidelines, but the elves want to be right in the middle of the action, showing off their moves by spinning and twirling gracefully.

Can you find Santa and the ten elves?

99

HOME SWEET HOME

Finally, the elves return home. They hadn't run away after all—they were gathering supplies to throw Santa the biggest and best party he's ever seen, to reward him for all his hard work.

It's too bad Santa's exhausted. He's fast asleep, snoring away.

Can you find a snoozing Santa and the ten elves partying with their friends?

France
Australia
Russia
Kenya
USA
England
Germany
Brazil

ANSWERS

Spotter's Checklist

Carol singers ☐

Someone falling through the ice ☐

A man dressed as a crocodile ☐

A badger ☐

Someone being hit in the face by a snowball ☐

A Snowy Village

Spotter's Checklist

A crocodile dentist ☐

A lion juggling an ornament ☐

A big cat pretending to be Rudolph ☐

A monkey with a bell ☐

An ostrich being ridden ☐

Safari Sensation

Spotter's Checklist

A man selling pretzels ☐

A skiier in the wrong place ☐

Two people dressed as snowmen ☐

A donkey sitting on a horse ☐

A man playing a tuba ☐

Christmas Market Mayhem

At the Beach

Spotter's Checklist

A platypus in a stocking ☐

A jellyfish on someone's head ☐

Ouch! Someone who's just sat on a porcupine ☐

A Santa kite ☐

A shark in a red cap ☐

Spotter's Checklist

A rocket-powered skiier ☐

Someone falling out of an elevator ☐

A human snowball ☐

Someone with two broken legs ☐

Someone skiing backward ☐

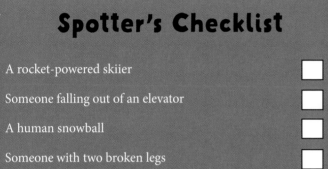

Alpine Adventure

Santas Galore

Spotter's Checklist

A reindeer who's reluctant to ride the escalator ☐

A Santa jumping into the pool ☐

A baby Santa ☐

An Easter Bunny Santa ☐

A Santa with a chimney on his head ☐

Spotter's Checklist

Someone dressed as a fairy ☐

Someone with an arrow on their forehead ☐

A girl wearing a fake mustache ☐

A stocking with a snowman ☐

Someone licking a candy cane ☐

Family Feast

At the Ballet

Spotter's Checklist

A vampire ☐

A dangling sandwich ☐

A pea shooter ☐

A pirate hat in the audience ☐

A telescope ☐

Spotter's Checklist

Someone doing the limbo ☐

A man with pineapples on his hat ☐

A gingerbread man ☐

A drummer with a whistle ☐

A trumpet player riding a horse ☐

Festive Fiesta!

Ice-Skating

Spotter's Checklist

A flying superhero ☐

A film crew ☐

Someone dressed as the Statue of Liberty ☐

An apple on ice skates ☐

Someone wearing a panda hat ☐

Spotter's Checklist

An elf skiing down the roof ☐

Two puppet elves ☐

An elf wearing a scuba mask ☐

A flying elf ☐

A snowboarding elf ☐

Home Sweet Home